Anonymous

Travellers' Guide

A complete list of the stations, distances & fares, from Portland, on the

railroads and steamboats in the state of Maine

Anonymous

Travellers' Guide
A complete list of the stations, distances & fares, from Portland, on the railroads and steamboats in the state of Maine

ISBN/EAN: 9783337410049

Printed in Europe, USA, Canada, Australia, Japan

Cover: Foto ©Andreas Hilbeck / pixelio.de

More available books at **www.hansebooks.com**

TRAVELLERS' GUIDE.

A COMPLETE LIST

OF THE

Stations, Distances & Fares,

FROM PORTLAND,

ON THE

RAILROADS AND STEAMBOATS

In the State of Maine. With other valuable information for Travellers.

PRICE 10 CENTS.

PORTLAND:
GEO. A. JONES & CO., PRINTERS.
1873.

HINTS TO RAILWAY TRAVELERS.

————o————

Passengers are bound to observe decorum in the cars, and are obliged to comply with all reasonable demands to show their tickets.

No passenger has a right to monopolize more seats than he has paid for.

Any article left in the seat, while the owner is temporarily absent, entitles him to the seat on his return.

Be careful to purchase tickets before entering the cars, thus avoiding much inconvenience.

Baggage, of ALL KINDS, should be checked.

Examine your checks, and be sure they are right, before leaving the Baggage Agent.

Railroad companies are not responsible for the loss of packages carried by passengers into the cars.

Be sure you get on the right car of the right train, before the time of starting, and thus save the annoyance of changing on the route, or the disappointment of reaching other than the desired station.

In addressing the Conductor on the train, do so, if possible, on his return, rather than when he is collecting tickets, as he then has little time to answer questions.

HINTS TO RAILWAY TRAVELERS.

————o————

In leaving a car, never attempt to get off before the train has come to a full stop ; but it is well to make some preparation previously, that there may be no delay after the train has stopped.

If, on arriving at your destination, you do not find your baggage, give a memorandum of your check, and description of the missing articles, to the Baggage Master, or Station Agent ; if it fails to reach you by succeeding trains, during the next twenty-four hours, apply to the Master of Passenger Transportation, informing him of all the facts, from which train missing, &c.

If, from any cause, it is needful to make complaint, do so to the chief of the department in which the grievance has occurred ; if no satisfaction is there obtained, then make a statement of the facts to the Superintendent ; but do not trouble either with fancied wrongs.

TREAT ALL WITH COURTESY, and you will receive it in return.

HINTS TO RAILWAY TRAVELERS.

————o————

You will save money by purchasing your Tickets before entering the cars.

CHECK YOUR BAGGAGE and the Company will then be responsible for it. Baggage in Passenger Cars is a source of anxiety to the owner; causes inconvenience to others; and is unsightly and altogether out of place.

Baggage can be checked THROUGH from places in Canada to the United States and VICE VERSA; but in such cases the law requires each Psssenger to point out his Baggage to the Customs' Officers at the Frontier Station, in order that it may be examined.

Avoid altercations with the Conductors or other Employees of the Company. Conductors have very responsible and arduous duties to perform on the journey, which require the utmost diligence on their part, and they have no time to enter into long discussion.

IT IS DANGEROUS to stand on the platform of cars or move from one car to another, or attempt to get on or off whilst the Train is in motion. Heads and arms are safest when they are INSIDE the car windows.

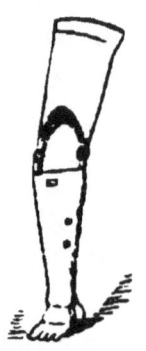

Eastern Railroad.

Connects with all Roads and Boats running North & East.

————o————

FROM PORTLAND.

FARES.		MILES.
$0 10	Cape Elizabeth	2
0 30	Oak Hill (Scarborough)	6
0 40	West Scarborough	9
0 55	Saco	13½
0 55	Biddeford	15
0 90	Kennebunk (Stage to Alfred)	23
1 15	Wells (Stage to Alfred)	28
1 25	North Berwick (Stage to Alfred)	34
1 40	South Berwick Junct.	38
1 50	Conway Junction	41
1 55	Elliot	45
1 65	Kittery	50½
1 65	Portsmouth	52
1 85	Greenland	57
1 95	North Hampton	59
2 05	Hampton	62
2 15	Hampton Falls	65
2 15	Seabrook	66
2 30	Salisbury	70
2 35	Newburyport	72
2 40	Knight's Crossing	74
2 55	Rowley	78
2 75	Ipswich	81
2 75	Wenham	86
2 80	North Beverly	88
2 85	Beverly	90
2 85	Salem	92
2 90	Swampscott	96
2 90	Lynn	97
2 90	West Lynn	98
2 90	Revere	102
2 90	Chelsea	104
2 90	Everett	105
3 00	Somerville	106
3 00	Boston	108

Portland and Ogdensburg Railroad.

—o—

From Portland.

FARES.		MILES.
$0 25	Stroudwater....................................	2½
0 35	Westbrook.....................................	5
0 50	South Windham................................	11
0 55	Gambo...	12
0 60	White Rock....................................	13½
0 75	Sebago Lake...................................	16¾
0 95	Richville.....................................	20½
1 10	Steep Falls...................................	21
1 20	East Baldwin..................................	26
1 30	Baldwin.......................................	29
	Stages daily for Cornish, Keazer Falls, Porter, and Freedom, N. H.	
1 45	West Baldwin..................................	33
1 55	Hiram...	36¼
1 85	Brownfield....................................	43
	Stages daily to Denmark and Bridgton.	
2 10	Fryeburg......................................	49
	Stages daily for Lovell and North Lovell.	
2 30	Center Conway, N. H.,.........................	55
2 50	North Conway, N. H.,..........................	60
	Discount of 10c. on Tickets bought at Stations.	

Portland and Rochester Railroad.

——o——

FROM PORTLAND.

FARES.		MILES.
$0 10	Morrill's	2½
0 25	Cumberland Mills	5
0 25	Saccarappa	6
0 35	Gorham	10
	Stages daily for West Gorham, Standish, & No. Limington.	
0 50	Buxton Center	15
	Stages daily for West Buxton, Bonny Eagle, and Limington.	
0 60	Saco River	18
	Stages tri-weekly for Limerick, Newfield, Adams' Corner, East Wakefield, Leighton's Corner, and Ossipee.	
0 70	Hollis Center	20½
0 90	Center Waterborough	25
	Stage Tuesday and tri-weekly for Limerick, Newfield, Parsonsfield, and Ossipee.	
1 00	So. Waterboro'	28
1 15	Alfred	32
1 30	Springvale	36½
	Stages daily for Shapleigh and No. Shapleigh.	
1 45	East Lebanon	42½
1 50	East Rochester	49½
1 50	Rochester (Junc. with D. & W. and P., G. F. & C. R. R.'s, for Boston, Lake Winnepisseogee and Conway.)	52½
3 00	Boston	

MASONIC MEETINGS

IN THE PRINCIPAL

TOWNS AND CITIES THROUGHOUT THE STATE.

———o———

BRIDGTON—Oriental, Saturday on or before full moon ; Oriental R. A. C., Thursday on or before full moon.

GORHAM—Harmon, Wednesday on or before full moon.

WESTBROOK—Temple, 4th Wednesday in month.

BUCKSPORT—Felicity, 1st Monday in month ; Hancock R. A. C., 1st Wednesday in month.

ELLSWORTH—Esoteric, 1st Friday in month ; Lygonia, Wednesday on or before full moon ; Acadia R. A. C., 1st Tuesday in mouth.

AUGUSTA—Augusta, Tuesday ; Bethlehem, first Monday.

GARDINER—Hermon, Tuesday on or before full moon ; Lonic, 1st Monday in month.

HALLOWELL—Kennebec, Wednesday on or before full moon ; Jerusalem R. A. C., Thursday on or before full moon.

WATERVILLE—Waterville, Monday on or before full moon.

CAMDEN—Amity, Friday on or before full moon ; Keystone R. A. C., 2d Wednesday of month.

ROCKLAND—Aurora, 1st Wednesday in month ; Rockland, 1st Tuesday in month ; King Solomon's Chapter, 1st Thursday in month ; King Hiram's Council, 1st Friday in mouth.

MASONIC MEETINGS

TOWNS AND CITIES THROUGHOUT THE STATE.

————o————

EASTPORT—Eastern, 1st Monday in month ; R. A. C., 1st Thursday in month ; K. T. C., 2d Tuesday in month.

ALFRED—Fraternal, Wednesday on or before full moon.

BIDDEFORD—Dunlap, No. 47, 1st Monday in month.

KENNEBUNK—York, Monday on or before full moon ; Murray R. A. C., Monday after full moon.

KENNEBUNKPORT--Arundel, Tuesday. .

SACO--York Chapter, 2d Wednesday in month ; Maine Council, 5th Wednesday in month ; Saco Lodge, 1st Wednesday in month.

SOUTH BERWICK—St. Johns, Monday on or before full moon ; Unity R. A. C., 1st Thursday in month.

————o————

KNIGHTS OF PYTHIAS.

Portland.—Place of meeting, Pythian Castle, No 8 Clapp's Block. Bramhall Lodge, No. 3, Thursday evenings ; Munjoy Lodge No. 6, Wednesday evenings.

Westbrook.—Presumpscot Valley, No. 4, Monday evenings.

Bangor —Norombega, No. 5.

MAINE CENTRAL RAILROAD.

Through Trains to Bangor.

————o————

Connects in Portland with Eastern, and Boston & Maine Railroads.

————o————

From Portland.

FARES.			MILES.
$0 15	Deering {	Woodford's......................	3
		Morrill's......................	5
0 30	West Falmouth.....................		9
0 40	Cumberland Junction...................		12
0 45	Yarmouth Junction, (G. T. R.)............		16
0 80	Freeport......................		22
1 25	Brunswick (Androscoggin R. R. connects....		30
1 40	Harding's......................		35
1 50	Bath (Knox & Lincoln R. R. connects)........		40
1 35	Topsham.......................		31
1 50	Bowdoinham......................		38
1 70	Harward's Road....................		41
1 85	Richmond......................		46
2 00	So. Gardiner.....................		51
2 10	Gardiner......................		56
2 20	Hallowell......................		61
2 25	Augusta......................		63
	Stages daily for Windsor, Liberty & Belfast.		
2 60	Seven Mile Brook...................		70
2 85	Vassalboro'......................		75
	Stages daily for East & No. Vassalboro', China.		
3 25	Winslow.......................		78
3 25	Waterville......................		81
3 35	Kendall's Mills....................		84
	Stages daily for Unity.		

MAINE CENTRAL RAILROAD.

Through Trains to Bangor continued.

Connects in Portland with Eastern and Boston & Maine Railroads.

FROM PORTLAND.

FARES.		MILES.
$3 50	Clinton	91¾
3 75	Burnham (Junc, B. & M. L. R. R,)	97
4 15	Unity	105
4 30	Thorndike	109
4 40	Brooks	119
4 50	City Point	129
4 50	Belfast	132
	Pittsfield	104
	Stages daily to Hartland, St. Albans, Athens, Harmony, Cambridge and Ripley.	
4 10	Detroit	108
4 25	Newport (N. & D, R. R.)	111
	Corinna	148
5 00	Dexter (daily Stage to Moosehead Lake,)	125
4 35	East Newport	113¾
	Stage daily to Plymouth and Dixmont.	
4 50	Etna	119½
	Stage daily to Stetson, Exeter and Levant.	
4 50	Carmel	123¼
4 50	Hermon Pond	127¾
	Stage to North Newburg.	
4 50	Bangor (E. & N. A. R. R. & B. & P. R. R.)	138
8 00	St. John, N. B	343½

Maine Central Railroad—Through Trains to Skowhegan.

Connects in Portland with Eastern, and Boston & Maine Railroad.

FARES.	FROM PORTLAND.	MILES.
$0 40	Cumberland Junction........................	12
0 55	Walnut Hill (No Yarmouth)...................	14
0 80	Perley's (Gray)............................	19
1 00	Chandler's (New Gloucester)................	22
1 10	Danville Junction (G. T. R.)..............	28
1 10	Auburn...................................	33½
	Stages daily to No. Auburn, Turner, North Turner, and Livermore Center.	
1 10	Lewiston..................................	34½
1 70	Greene...................................	42
	Daily Stage to South Leeds.	
1 80	Leeds (Junc. A. R. R.).....................	45½
1 90	Monmouth.................................	48¼
2 00	Winthrop..................................	54
	Stages daily to Augusta and Manchester.	
2 25	Readfield.................................	60
	Stages daily to Kent's Hill, Vienna, Mount Vernon, Farmington and Farmington Falls.	
2 50	Belgrade..................................	68
	Stages daily to New Sharon, Mercer, East New Sharon, Rome, and Smithfield.	
2 70	No. Belgrade..............................	72¼
2 95	West Waterville...........................	76½
3 25	Waterville................................	83
	Stages daily to Fairfield, No. Fairfield, Larone and So. Norridgewock.	
3 35	Kendall's Mills...........................	86
	Stage daily for Unity and Benton.	
3 40	Somerset Mills............................	85
3 55	Pishon's Ferry............................	92
	Stages daily to Canaan.	
4 00	Skowhegan................................	100
	Stages daily to Norridgewock, No. Anson, New Portland, Solon, Athens, and Harmony.	

JOSEPH CRAIG.　　　　CHARLES JACKSON.　　　　SAMUEL H. BRACKETT.

CRAIG, JACKSON & BRACKETT,

PLASTERERS,

Plain and Ornamental Stucco and Mastic Workers,

NO. 29 PLEASANT STREET.

PORTLAND, ME.

Prompt attention paid to Whitening, Whitewashing & Coloring.

GRAND TRUNK RAILWAY.

—o—

Connects in Portland with Eastern, and Boston & Maine Railroads from Boston.

—o—

FROM PORTLAND.

FARES.		MILES.
$0.30	Falmouth	5½
0 45	Cumberland	8⅛
0 50	Yarmouth	11¼
0 50	Yarmouth Junction (P. & K. R. R.)	12⅛
0 70	No. Yarmouth	15¼
	Stage daily to Pownal and Durham.	
0 80	Pownal	18½
1 00	New Gloucester	22⅝
	Stage daily to Upper and West Gloucester, No. Raymond, and So. Poland.	
1 10	Danville Junction (M. C. R. R.)	27½
1 30	Hotel Road	28¾
1 40	Empire Road	32
1 60	Mechanic Falls (Junc. P. & Oxford Central Railroad)	36¼
	Daily Stage to Poland and West Poland.	
1 70	Oxford	40¾
	Stage Monday and tri-weekly to Casco, Naples, and Otisfield.	
1 95	So. Paris	47¼
	Stage daily to Paris, Norway, Bridgton, and Harrison; Monday and tri-weekly to Waterford and Lovell.	
2 20	West Paris	55⅝
	Stage daily to No. Paris and Woodstock.	
2 50	Bryant's Pond	61¾
	Stage daily to Rumford; Monday and tri-weekly to Andover; Tuesday and tri-weekly to Rumford Center, Peru and Dixfield.	

BAILEY & NOYES, Piano Forte Warerooms,

GREAT REDUCTION

PRICES! IN

All who desire to purchase a Chickering Piano will please read the following:

By abolishing all discounts, Messrs. Chickering & Son have abandoned the old style of Piano selling, and adopted in its place the One Price system. Every Instrument, WHEREVER SOLD, bears invariably the fixed price. Messrs. Bailey & Noyes are now authorized to sell an elegant Rosewood Seven Octave Chickering Piano, for

$475 !!

The price for the same instrument under the old system of discounts, was $600. The same scale of great reduction in ALL CLASSES OF THEIR INSTRUMENTS.

Particular attention is called to the fact that the LARGEST STOCK OF PIANOS kept in the State, will be found at our warerooms. Instruments will be sold on installments, if desired, giving persons of moderate means an opportunity to buy; and prices are so exceedingly low, ranging from $50 upward, that all who choose may enjoy one of these indispensable ministers of social happiness.

BUSINESS LAW.

—— o——

It is not legally necessary to say on a note "for value received."

A note drawn on Sunday is void.

A note obtained by fraud, or from an intoxicated person, cannot be collected.

If a note be lost or stolen, it does not release the maker ; he must pay it.

An endorser of a note is exempt from liability if not served with notice of its dishonor within twenty-four hours of its non-payment.

A note given by a minor is void.

Notes bear interest only when so stated.

Principals are responsible for the acts of their agents.

Each individual in a partnership is responsible for the whole amount of the debts of a firm.

Ignorance of the law excuses no one.

It is a fraud to conceal a fraud.

The law compels no one to do impossibilities.

An agreement without a consideration is void.

Signatures made with a lead pencil are good in law

A Receipt for money paid is not legally conclusive.

The acts of one partner bind all the others.

MAXIMS

FOR EVERYBODY.

Never fail to take a receipt for money paid, and keep copies of your letters.

Do your business promptly and bore not a business man with long visits.

Law is a trade in which the lawyers eat the oysters and leave the clients the shells.

Caution is the father of security.

He who pays before-hand is served behind-hand.

If you would know the value of a dollar try to borrow one.

No man can be successful who neglects his business.

Be silent when a fool talks.

Give a foolish talker rope enough and he will hang himself.

Never speak boastingly of your business.

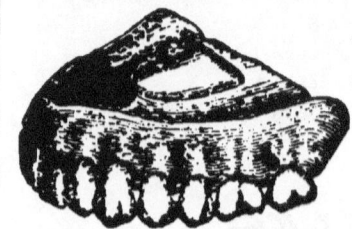

Drs. JOHNSON & FRENCH,

DENTISTS,

Office over H. H. Hay's Apothecary Store,

JUNCTION OF FREE & MIDDLE STS.

Drs. J. & F. have all necessary facilities for preparing *Pure Nitrous Oxide (Laughing Gas.)* The *best Preparation* that can be *taken* so that *Teeth* can be *Extracted without pain.*

They claim to *fill teeth* in the best possible manner, *Teeth* that are *half* or *two-thirds* gone by *decay,* they can build up with Gold so as to render them serviceable for years.

Artificial Teeth, from one to a full set, on the Vulcanized Rubber, Gold or *Silver* are *fitted* by *them,* and warranted to be as perfect as can possibly be made, and to give entire *satisfaction* to the *patient.*

They will administer *Ether* to those who prefer it to the Gas.

They cordially solicit the patronage of persons desiring skilfully performed Dental operations.

WALTER R. JOHNSON,   ALGER W. FRENCH.

VALUE OF FOREIGN MONEY.

On a Gold Basis.

——o——

Pound Sterling, of England,	-	-	$ 4.84
Guinea, "	-	-	5.05
Crown, "	-	-	1.21
Shilling, "	-	-	.22
Napoleon, of France,	-	-	3 84
Five Francs, "	-	-	.93
Franc, "	-	-	.18½
Thaler, of Saxony,	-	-	.68
Guilder, of Netherlands,	-	-	.40
Ducat, of Austria,	-	-	2.28
Florin, "	-	-	.48½
Doubloon, of Spain (1800),	-	-	15.54
Real. "	-	-	.05
Five Rubles, of Russia,	-	-	8.95
Ruble, "	-	-	.75
Franc, of Belgium,	-	-	.18½
Ducat, of Bavaria,	-	-	2.27
Franc, of Switzerland,	-	-	.18½
Crown, of Tuscany,	-	-	1.05½

———◆•◆•◆———

ADVICE IN CASES OF POISONING.

——o——

Stir into a glass of water a heaping teaspoonful each of salt and mustard and drink immediately. One or more doses will cause vomiting, and cleanse the stomach. To overcome 'the effects, swallow the whites of two or three eggs, and drink a cup or two of strong coffee.

Sweet Oil, taken freely, is excellent in poisoning.

MONEY-ORDER OFFICES IN MAINE,

Alfred,
Auburn,
Augusta,
Bangor,
Bath,
Belfast,
Bethel,
Biddeford,
Boothbay,
Brewer,
Bridgton,
Brunswick,
Buckfield,
Bucksport,
Calais,
Camden,
Castine,
Cherryfield.
Dexter,
East Machias,

Eastport,
Ellsworth,
Farmington,
Fort Fairfield,
Foxcroft,
Fryeburg,
Gardiner,
Gorham,
Houton
Kendall's Mills
Lubec,
Lewiston,
Machias,
Mechanic Falls
Newport,
New Sharon,
Norway,
Paris,
Pembroke,
Phillips,

Portland,
Presque Isle,
Richmond,
Rockland,
Saco,
Solon,
Searsport,
Skowhegan,
South Berwick,
Springvale,
Stockton,
Thomaston,
Unity,
Waldoborough,
Waterville,
Wilton,
Winterport,
Winthrop,
Wiscasset,
Yarmouth.

INTERNATIONAL MONEY OFFICES.

Augusta,
Bangor,
Bath,
Belfast,
Brunswick,
Calais.

Eastport,
Ellsworth,
Houlton,
Lewiston,
Portland,

Rockland,
Saco,
South Berwick,
Thomaston,
Yarmouth,

MONEY ORDERS

Between the United Kingdom of Great Britain,
German Empire, Switzerland, and the
United States.

———o———

On orders not exceeding $5 (to German
   Empire)   -   -   -   -   15 cts.
On orders not exceeding $10 -   -   25 "
Over $10 and not exceeding $20,   -   50 "
Over $20 and not exceeding $30,   -   75 "
Over $30 and not exceeding $40,   - $1 00 "
Over $40 and not exceeding $50,   -   1 25 "
United States Treasury notes or National Bank notes
   only received or paid.

REGISTRY DEPARTMENT.

———o———

Letters may be registered by paying postage in
full, and a registration fee in stamps, for—
United States,   -   -   -   15 cts.
Canada, New Brunswick, Nova Scotia and
   New Foundland,   -   -   -   5 "
England, Ireland and Scotland,   -   8 "
German-Austrian Postal Union, embracing
   the German and Austrian States,   -   8 "
Spain and Portugal,   -   -   16 "
Belgium and Holland,   -   -   8 "
France,   -   -   -   -   8 "

Knox & Lincoln Railroad.

———o———

FROM PORTLAND.

FARES.		MILES.
$1 50	Bath	40
1 55	Woolwich	41
1 65	Nequasset	43½
1 75	Montsweag	46½
1 75	Wiscasset	51¼
2 00	Newcastle and Damariscotta	58½

Stages daily for Bristol and Pemoquid.

2 10	Damariscotta Mills	60½
2 20	Nobleboro'	63
2 25	Winslow's Mills	68¼
2 25	Waldoboro'	70¼
2 50	Warren	77

Stages Monday, Wednesday, and Friday, to
Union, Jefferson, and Whitefield.

2 50	George's River	82½
2 50	Thomaston	85

Stage daily for St. George.

2 50	Rockland	89

Stages daily to Camden, Lincolnville, North-
port, St. George's, and So. Thomaston;
Tuesdays, Thursdays, and Fridays, for
Union, Appleton, and Washington. Steam-
ers for all Points on the Penobscot River,
Hurricane and Dix Islands.

4

European & North American Railway.

FROM PORTLAND.

Fares fm Bangor.	FARES.		MILES.
		Bangor, M. C. Depot	138
		Exchange Street	138½
		Mount Hope	140
$0 20		Veazie	142¾
0 35		Basin Mills	145½
0 35		Eight Mile Siding	146
0 35	$4 75	Orono	146½
0 45		Great Works	149½
0 50	4 90	Oldtown (Junc. B. & P. R. R.)	150½
0 50		Milford	151½
0 75		Costigan	156⅜
1 00		Greenbush	161
1 25		Olaman	164¾
1 45	5 85	Passadumkeag	169
1 65		Enfield	173
2 00	6 40	Lincoln	182¾
2 00		Lincoln Centre	184⅙
2 50	6 90	Winn	193½
2 60	7 00	Mattawaumkeag	196
2 85	7 25	Kingman	204
3 05		Bancroft	217
3 30		Danforth	226
3 35		Jackson Brook	231
3 70		Lambert Lake	247
3 75	8 00	Vanceboro'	252
3 75	8 00	St. Croix, N. B.	252
3 95	8 00	McAdam Junc. (Junc. N. B. & C. R. R.)	258
4 95	8 00	Fredrickton Junc. (Junc. F. B. R. R.)	297½
6 00	8 00	St. John, N. B.	343½

St. Croix & Penobscot Railroad.

FROM CALAIS.

Stages to Eastport and intermediate towns.

FARES.		MILES.
$0 05	Milltown	2
0 15	Baring	5
0 40	Sprague's Falls	10
0 50	Whidden's Farm	13
0 65	Baileyville	18
0 75	Princeton	21

Stage to Grand Lake Stream, Topsfield, pringfield, Jackson Brook, &c.

Portland, Bangor & Machias Steamboat Line.

———o———

INSIDE OR BANGOR ROUTE.

Leaves Railroad Wharf on arrival of steamboat train Boston.

FROM PORTLAND.

FARES.		MILES.
$1 50	Rockland	80
1 50	Camden	88
1 50	Lincolnville	97
2 00	Belfast	106
2 00	Searsport	113
2 50	Bucksport	122
2 50	Winterport	127
2 50	Hamden	134
2 50	Bangor	140

MACHIAS & MT. DESERT ROUTE.

$3 00	Castine		110
3 00	Deer Isle		130
3 00	Sedgwick		132
4 00	Mount Desert	So. West Harbor	155
5 00		Bar Harbor	170
5 00	Millbridge		207
5 00	Jonesport		222
5 00	Machiasport		250

———

Portland Steam Packet Company.

———o———

DAILY LINE OF FIRST-CLASS STEAMERS BETWEEN BOSTON AND PORTLAND.

Steamers leave Atlantic Wharf, Portland, and India Wharf, Boston, every evening (Sundays excepted), at 7 P. M.

From middle of September to middle of April, the hour of leaving Boston is 5 P. M.

FARE, $1.50. From Portland about 112 miles. State-rooms $1.00.

International Steamship Company.

Steamboats leave Central Wharf, Portland, Mondays at 6 o'clock in January and February; Mondays and Thursdays in March, April, May, June, October, November and December; Mondays, Wednesdays and Fridays, at six o'clock in July, August and September.

Exact running time somewhat dependent upon time of arrival of trains from Boston. Number of boats each week somewhat dependent upon business and opening of navigation.

FARES.	FROM PORTLAND.	MILES.
$3 50	Eastport, - - -	180
4 00	Calais, - - -	213
	connects with Steamer for Calais.	
4 50	St. John, - - -	250
	State-rooms $2 00 extra.	

Sanford's Independent Line of Steamers.

FARES.	FROM BANGOR.	MILES.
$0 50	Hamden	6
0 75	Winterport	13
0 65	Bucksport	18
1 00	Searsport	27
1 00	Belfast, (M. C. R, R.)	34
1 50	Camden	52
1 50	Rockland (K. & L. R. R)	60
4 00	Boston, Mass	235

Kennebec Steamboat Company.

FARES.	FROM AUGUSTA.	MILES.
$	Hollowell	2
0 25	Gardiner	6
0 25	Richmond	17
0 50	Bath	32
2 00	Boston	165

Leaves Kennebec River Mondays and Thursdays, and Boston Tuesdays and Fridays, during the season of open navigation.

Máine Steamship Company.

New York Steamers leave Galt's Wharf, Portland, every Monday and Thursday at 4 o'clock, P. M., in winter, and 5 o'clock, P. M., in summer, and New York the same day at 3 o'clock, P. M., in winter, and 4 o'clock, P. M,, in summer.

FARE, $5.00, including berth in State-room, meals extra.

———o———

New England and Nova Scotia Steamship Company.

Steamers leave Galt's Wharf every Saturday, at at 4 o'clock, P. M., for Halifax in winter; in summer on Tuesdays and Saturdays, at 5.30 P. M.

FARE, $7.00, Stateroom, meals extra.

———o———

Damariscotta and Waldoborough Steamboat Company.

Steamer Charles Houghton leaves Atlantic Wharf during the season of open navigation, Wednesday mornings for Boothbay, Round Pond and Waldoboro'; Saturday mornings for Boothbay, Hodgdon's Mills and Damariscotta. Returning, leaves Damariscotta on Monday, and Waldoboro' on Friday.

U. S. POSTAGE.

———o———

All postage must be prepaid, by affixing stamps denoting the postage required, upon letters, packages, or other mail matter.

Every letter, or written communication, weight not over half an ounce, any distance within the United States, 3 cents; for each additional half ounce, or fraction, 3 cents in addition.

Manuscripts, for Newspapers, and Magazines, letter rates.

Drop Letters, 1 cent for every half ounce or less. At offices where free delivery by carrier is established. 2 cents for each half ounce.

Postal Cards, with stamp impressed, one cent each.

Pamphlets, occasional publications, transient newspapers, magazines and periodicals, hand-bills, posters, sheet-music, unsealed circulars, prospectuses, book manuscripts and proof-sheets, printed cards, maps, lithographs, prints, chromo-lithographs and engravings, seeds, cuttings, bulbs, roots and scions, 1 cent for each two ounces or fraction thereof; weight of packages limited to four pounds.

Flexible Patterns, samples of ores, metals, minerals and merchandise, sample cards, phonographic paper, letter envelopes, postal envelopes and wrappers, unprinted cards, plain and ornamental paper, photographs and all other articles for which other rates of postage are not prescribed in this table, and which are not by law excluded from the mails, 2 cents for each two ounces or fraction thereof; weight of packages limited to 12 ounces.

U. S. POSTAGE—Continued.

———o———

Books, 2 cents for each two ounces or fraction thereof ; weight of packages limited to four pounds.

Weekly Newspapers, Postage must be paid quarterly in advance, as follows : Weekly papers, 5 cents ; semi-weekly, 10 cents ; tri-weekly, 15 cents, and so on, adding 5 cents for each additional issue.

Quarterly Magazines, &c., 1 cent per quarter for every 4 ounces thereof ; monthly, three times, semi-monthly six times this rate.

Religious, Educational, and Agricultural Newspapers, of small size, issued less frequently than once a week, may be sent in packages to one address at the rate of 1 cent for each package not exceeding four ounces in weight, and an additional charge of 1 cent is made for each additional four ounces or fraction thereof, the postage to be paid quarterly or yearly in advance.

News Dealers may receive and send periodicals to regular subscribers, as publishers, but packages so sent cannot be returned except by pre-payment of transient rates.

Franking Privilege, repealed after July 1, 1873.

Money Orders from $1 to $ 50, may be obtained at any post-office in the United States authorized to transact this business. Commission charged for transmitting sums from $1 to $10, 5 cents ; from $10 to $20, 10 cents ; over $20 and not exceeding $30, 15 cents ; over $30 and not exceeding $40, 20 cents ; over $40 and not exceeding $50, 25 cents. Not over three orders can be sent at one time.

DISTANCES FROM PORTLAND

To the largest Towns in each State.

———o———

	MILES.
Washington, D. C. - - -	554
Concord, N. H. - - -	111
Montpelier, Vt. - - -	150
Boston, Mass. - - -	118
Providence, R. I. - - -	153
Hartford, Conn. - - -	218
New York, N. Y. - - -	341
Trenton, N. J. - - -	401
Philadelphia, Pa. - - -	431
Wilmington, Del. - - -	559
Baltimore, Md. - - -	559
Richmond, Va. - - -	719
Raleigh, N. C. - - - -	842
Charleston, S. C. - - -	1098
Savannah, Ga. - - - -	1211
Cahawba, Ala. - - -	1469
Monticello, Miss. - - -	1784
New Orleans, La. - - -	1814
Murfreesboro, Tenn. - - -	1262
Frankfort, Ky. - - -	1119
Columbus, Ohio. - - -	852
Indianapolis, Ind. - - -	1064
Vandalia, Ill. - . - -.	1292
St. Louis, Mo. - - -	1331

POPULAR RESORTS.

And other places of Interest in the vicinity of the city
of Portland, and their distances, making
the head of Free Street the
starting point.

———o———

To Libby's at Prouts neck, by way of Broad's,	13½
" Same—by way of Vaughn's Bridge, old road,	11
" Atlantic House, Scarborough, by way of Vaughn's Bride,	10
" Kirkwood House,	10
" Reform School,	4
" White House,	3
" Ocean House, Bowery Beach,	8
" First of the two Cape Lights,	8½
" Cape Cottage,	3½
" Evergreen Cemetery, following the Horse Railroad Track,	3
" Marine Hospital,	2¾
From head of Cape Elizabeth ferryways to Cape Cottage,	2½
" Ocean House to Libby's, Prout's Neck,	7½
" Union Wharf to Diamond Cove is about,	5
To Pleasant Cove,	5
" Peake' Island Landing,	3
" White Head,	3½
" Cape Cottage,	3½
" Forest or Clapboard Island,	7
" Basket Island,	8
" Jewell's Island,	9½
" Goose Island, (Crouch's Cove,)	17